Tales From

LaMPLIGHT LaNe

Book 1

SQUID

Darren S. Philibert

Whimsical Publications, LLC

Florida

Tales from Lamplight Lane: Squid is a work of fiction. Names, characters, and incidents are the products of the author's imagination and are either fictitious or are used fictitiously. Any resemblance to actual events or persons, living or dead, is entirely coincidental.

To purchase the authorized electronic edition of
Tales from Lamplight Lane: Squid, visit
www.whimsicalpublications.com

Cover art by Janet Durbin
Editing by Brieanna Robertson

ISBN-13: 978-1-63495-020-6

Published by
Whimsical Publications, LLC
Florida

acknowledgement

Special thanks to all my awesome friends who were the inspiration for some of the characters and these stories: Travis Lovett, Tylisha Ruffin, Loren Cox, Johnny Jones. And to my amazing and supportive wife Tara for putting up with me.

THE
PACIFIC
NORTHWEST
GIANT
LUMINESCENT
FRESHWATER
SQUID

recommendations BY THE author:

1. Before reading, it is recommended that you take everything that you know is normal, standard, average, and scientifically sound and toss it out the window. That way of thinking will only frustrate and confuse you.

2. It is also highly recommended that you read in the voice of John Cleese, a famous British actor. This will make the story much more enjoyable and clever sounding. (If you really needed me to explain who John Cleese was, shame on you!)

3. And, finally, it is very highly recommended that you enjoy the story. Because if you don't then all this would be for nothing and we will all end up looking like fools (but mostly me).

Now, get into your favorite chair, brew up your favorite tea, and hold all your questions until after the story has finished. Cheers!

TABLE OF CONTENTS

1

INTRODUCTIONS

Have you ever seen the Great Pacific Northwest Giant Luminescent Freshwater Squid? Few have. In fact, only four young children have ever laid eyes on such a creature, and boy do they have a whopper of a story to tell. So if you enjoy whopper-esque stories, you've come to the right place. If not, well then we can't all be as sophisticated as you, now can we? Now that I've given you fair warning, I believe some introductions are in order.

THE TOWN

Lamplight Lane was so named because one day at the end of fall, an enormous swarm of fireflies caravanned through town, and at that moment, winter struck like a viper. The little glowing insects were instantly frozen. They fell to the ground, lighting the way through town as permanent tiny street lamps. Amazing things happen in Lamplight Lane on a daily basis, ranging from mutant sheep to wormholes. Which, actually now that I think about it, happened the same day. When mutant sheep started terrorizing the town, a small localized wormhole materialized in town square and sucked the sheep into oblivion, and thus one problem became the solution to the other. And the inhabitants of Lamplight Lane were just as peculiar as the town itself.

FrancIS MUCK

The leader of the gang. What gang, you ask? Well, just hang on. I'm not finished telling about poor Francis Muck yet. Yes *poor* Francis Muck. Why poor, you ask? My, aren't you the curious type. Well, poor Francis Muck was known as the boy who always lost, because just as the title says he *always* lost. Whether it be cards, chess, baseball, or a staring contest with a mirror, the end result would always be the same. The whole Muck family were losers really, but not in the same way Francis was a loser, if you catch my drift. Even though Francis Muck didn't have much luck (hmm that's catchy) he did have friends.

CLYDE MCGEE

The boy who could change into anything. If you need more of an explanation, then I feel very sorry for you. Clyde was a crafty lad, always coming up with bad schemes and poorly executed stunts. For example, Clyde once "forgot" to do a report on the migratory patterns of June Bugs and so changed into his report and handed himself in for a grade. It would have worked except that when the teacher came to Clyde's report to grade it, as soon as she started to write the grade on it, it tickled Clyde something fierce. He started giggling, and with a *POP,* sitting there on Mrs. Poole's desk was Clyde McGee with an A+ on his forehead. Mrs. Poole promptly reached up and crossed out the A and wrote an F. Things only got worse after he tried to simultaneously change into himself and his mother and father for the parent/teacher conference thereafter.

rePTILe raLF

So nicknamed for his love of reptiles and his curious ability to summon them to do his bidding (or it could be his scaly greenish skin, not sure which really). Ralf converted his entire backyard into a reptile kingdom. His parents allowed this only if he took responsibility to care for the creatures. That ... and that he would not command an alligator to eat them.

Last and, in this case least as well, is...

PaLYN SKINNY

I really to the 10th power wish I could embellish this and put a positive spin on it, but there's no getting around it. Palyn Skinny is eye-gougingly, gut-wrenchingly and bowel-loosingly ugly (bowl-loosingly: now a recognized word in Webster's Dictionary thanks to Palyn). He is such a bad eyesore that town hall pays him to stand next to the town's landfill so as to make it more pleasant looking. Nowadays, Palyn wears an old rice sack over his head with two eyeholes cut out to spare the town folk from having to look upon his grotesque features.

Thus as you can imagine our four friends have many wondrous stories to tell.

...so where were we? Ah yes, the Pacific Northwest Giant Luminescent Freshwater Squid...

2

Brainstorm

Sitting outside on his front porch, Francis Muck held in his hand Lamplight Lane's newspaper, *The Lamp Post*. His eyes bulged out at an ad for a photography contest at this year's Pepper Festival. Lamplight Lane was known for its pepper plants and their production, thus making it the town's most beloved spice. Every year the town got together and celebrated their pepper heritage by having contests, games, and entertainment of all sorts. One of the most popular games was the Sneeze Olympics. Contests in the Sneeze Olympics ranged from the Sneez-athalon, where contestants competed for loudest, most powerful and most original sneeze, to the Last Man Sneezing contest, where competitors saw who could sneeze the longest repeatedly without throwing up, passing out, or popping out an eyeball. Francis stared at the newspaper, imagining himself winning the photography contest and having his photo put on a stamp. The grand prize for the photography contest was four dollars!

Wait a minute, sorry, Francis was so excited about this he'd drooled on the newspaper, covering the two zeros. It was actually four *hundred* dollars. But who was Francis kidding? He never won anything. There must be a way he could win.

An idea came to him like a flash of lightning. A moment later, Francis woke up on the ground, slightly toasted but with a grand idea. *Sheesh!* Francis thought. *That's the sixth time this year. I should really start thinking indoors more, and on less cloudy days.* The words "Old Man Groys" escaped his lips along with a small puff of smoke.

3

ZZZZZZZZT!

Lightning is an atmospheric discharge of electricity, which typically occurs during thunderstorms, and sometimes during volcanic eruptions or dust storms.

NOTE This chapter, although very interesting, is incredibly boring. It is recommended you just skip to chapter four. **NOTE**

In the atmospheric electrical discharge, a leader of a bolt of lightning can travel at speeds of 60,000 m/s, and can reach temperatures approaching 30,000 °C (54,000 °F), hot enough to fuse silica sand into petrified lightning, known scientifically as glass channels or fulgurites which are normally hollow and can extend some distance into the ground. There are some 16 million lightning storms in the world every year. For an American, the chance of being struck by lightning are approximately 576,000 to 1 and the chance of actually being killed by lightning is approximately 2,320,000 to 1.

Lightning can also occur within the ash clouds from

volcanic eruptions, or can be caused by violent forest fires, which generate sufficient dust to create a static charge.

How lightning initially forms is still a matter of debate. Scientists have studied root causes ranging from atmospheric perturbations (wind, humidity, friction, and atmospheric pressure) to the impact of solar wind and accumulation of charged solar particles. Ice inside a cloud is thought to be a key element in lightning development, and may cause a forcible separation of positive and negative charges within the cloud, thus assisting in the formation of lightning.

In case you actually read this detailed explanation about the wonders of nature and science, let me just say that...wow...I am actually impressed. Your sixth-grade science teacher would be proud!

THE STORY WEAVER

Old man Groys spun stories much like a spider spins a web (In fact he actually spun a real web once, but that's another story we'll save for later). They start with an outlying structure and give the stories a good foundation and beginning, but soon become an intricate and interwoven conundrum that seems to have no set pattern. Then, ever so slowly, the web begins to take shape. When finished, if you step back and take it all in, you see that it's really quite an impressive work of art, and that is the art of storytelling. Groys was the type of crazy old coot that couldn't even find his elbows on a daily basis. But when it came to weaving a story, there was just no comparison.

This was Francis' idea. Well, I should say this was part of Francis's idea. He figured he would get the gang to help him out with the rest of it. Groys was a goldmine of stories, tales, and legends. He also smelled of cottage cheese.

Francis' half idea was this: He would simply ask Groys to tell him about some of the amazing local legends and see which one would present the best photo opportunity. Then once he had his photograph of Big-foot's cousin or whatever, he would win the contest for sure. Now it was time to collect the gang and get over to Old Man Groys' place. Fame, fortune, and four hundred dollars awaited Francis.

5

NO HESITATION FORMING THE AWAY TEAM

BANG! BOOM! CRASH! ROOOAARR! AHHHH! Clyde couldn't take it anymore. He reached up and turned off the TV. He was watching the sci-fi movie of the week. It was about a giant petrified wooly mammoth that was found in some tar pits and was brought back to life, then proceeded to run amuck through a local town. In the end, it was taken out by a tornado machine that a brilliant local scientist invented and sucked the mammoth into outer space. Clyde thought this was ridiculous. That was nothing like what happened. It was in fact a giant *sloth,* not a mammoth. Ridiculous. He really wished Hollywood would write their own material sometimes.

The sound of a buzzer cleared the hatred for overpaid movie directors out of Clyde's head. He reached over and flipped a switch to a monitor and saw that Francis was standing outside his house. He then pulled on a large lever that set in motion a whole lot of things at once. Gears turned, wires contorted, and pulleys...well...pulled. Then on the outside of Clyde's house, a bush right next to where Francis was standing slid over and uncovered a submarine-like hatch in the ground. The hatch unlocked with a whooshing sound, and Francis opened the lid the rest of the way and jumped in, slamming the lid behind him.

Two point three seconds later, Francis slid out of a doggy door in the basement wall of Clyde's room. Francis, never skipping a beat, ran over and plopped down on the couch next to Clyde, who was now in the form of Leonard Nimoy, TV's Spock from *Star Trek.*

"Hey, wanna get Groys to tell us about some crazy legend and try to track it down so we can get an amazing photo of it and enter it into the photo contest at the Pepper Festival and possibly even get our faces on a stamp?" asked Francis.

Mr. Nimoy turned to Francis, holding his hand up in the Live Long and Prosper sign, and said, "That seems logical, count me in." Clyde never needed any convincing; he was always ready to go within a second's notice. In fact, one time Francis asked Clyde if he wanted to help him climb Mt. Slaughterdoom# to build an observatory. (The observatory was to serve as a town defense against alien invasion. As soon as the last stone was placed, it immediately collapsed in a huge pile of rubble. Apparently, just watching a TV show on how to build a shed didn't provide enough knowhow to build an observatory. Amazingly, what Francis and Clyde never knew was that during the structure's collapse, it just so happened to crush and kill a cloaked alien reconnaissance scout for an invading alien armada. The alien army figured that if this species could so easily take out a highly trained and almost undetectable scout, they were simply no match for such an advanced civilization and called the whole invasion off. So, unknown to Francis, and the entire earth, his observatory actually accomplished what is was originally purposed to do). So before Francis was even finished saying the word observatory, Clyde was already packing.

Much the same this time, Mr. Nimoy was already putting on his jacket, which was way too small for him. After changing back into himself, Clyde put on his jacket with success and they were off to get Palyn and Ralf.

#*Mt. Slaughterdoom was first explored and founded in 1920 by Edward Slaughterdoom. The mountain itself is actually a rather easy climb, and many families hike this pristine mountain for picnics in the summer.*

6

even MIKe rowe WOULDN'T TOUCH THIS DIrTY JOB

The horrible stench filled both Francis and Clyde's nostrils as they walked down the street. Following the putrid smell, they finally arrived at their destination—the town's most beautiful landfill. Standing there next to it was Palyn Skinny.

A sad sight he was. Just to looking at him for more than a few seconds would make one's eyes start to water. Any longer than that and he would make their stomach turn. Francis and Clyde came up to Palyn with their heads lowered, so as to avoid vomiting.

"Hey, Palyn, man, the landfill is looking good today!" commented Clyde.

"What can I say, I'm good at what I do," said Palyn.

"Say, we are headed over to old man Groys' place for a tale of epic proportions. It's part of a project I'm working on, and we could use some help. Wanna join us?" asked Francis.

"Ya, sure. I'm off now anyways." Palyn picked up a sign with a pointed end on it and jammed it into the ground. It read: Sorry Landfill Closed—Come see us to-morrow. He then grabbed his old rice bag and fitted it over his head. He lined up the eyeholes and set off to get Ralf.

7

IT'S NATURE, IT'S NOT SUPPOSED TO BE PRETTY

I feel it's fair to warn you that if you are afraid of things that slither, claw, and bite, you might want to close your eyes while you read this part. Although that might make it a tad hard to read anything at all. So here is what I will recommend. Simply close your eyes, lift your index finger, and drop it down onto the page below and start reading from there on. You may miss some things, but it's okay. I'm sure you'll get the gist later on.

Slythe's tongue flickered in Ralf's ear to tell him of people approaching. Slythe was a giant Boa Constrictor. Ralf would have Slythe pick him up in his massive muscular coil in a sort of living scale throne. Ralf looked down to see his friends walking up to the base of Slythe's coils. In every direction the three others looked, they saw snakes, lizards, turtles, alligators, and crocodiles. Ralf's reptile kingdom was a thing of terrifying beauty. The three never really got used to it, though. Eager to leave the vicinity and get to Groys' place, they told Ralf of the plan and he agreed to leave with them right after he finished one minor task. He had Slythe put him on the ground. Then he walked over to the back door of his house and up into his arms leapt a little white poodle. He handed it to Francis to hold for him while he closed the back door.

Francis gently stroked the cute poodle's curly fur while it looked up at him with big soulful eyes and timidly licked him on the nose.

Ralf then took the poodle from Francis' arms with a "thanks" and thusly flung the poodle high into the air over a large pool. With amazing aquatic acrobatics breeched Harriet, a gigantic freshwater crocodile, that deftly snapped up the poodle in one bite*. The other three stood with eyes wide in shock and jaws to the floor. Ralf turned around with a broad smile. "Isn't nature amazing!"

*Poodles: Nature's Hors D'oeuvres

8

PICK a STOrY, aNY STOrY

After having their fill of nature, the gang finally arrived at old man Groys' house. They walked up onto the front porch and came up to his door. They knocked loudly, knowing that Groys was practically deaf and they would have to knock several more times. KNOCK, KNOCK, KNOCK!

From inside they heard shuffling and movement, then a yowl from what clearly sounded like a cat being stepped on. Which was strange because Groys didn't have a cat. After about twenty minutes, Groys emerged from his house. Being a man of routine (and being half blind as well), he took two steps forward and then turned to his left and then took four more steps forward, turned to his right and ever so slowly inched down into his old rocking chair.

The kids knew the routine all too well. They simply waited for him to do what he did. He settled into his chair and then withdrew an old corncob pipe. After packing it, he lit it up and sat back in his chair, beginning to rock comfortably. After a few minutes of silence, he raised his brow with what looked like a lot of effort and peered out to see the boys patiently waiting there for him.

"Well now, what's it gunna be today, boys? You wanna hear about the time they found a petrified mammoth in the tar pits..."

"Sloth," corrected a slightly irritated Clyde.

"No, we know that one. What else you got?" said Francis.

Groys' brow furrowed as he thought back. "How about the mysterious tale of the ghost of Lamplight Dan?"

The boys looked at each other questioningly.

"Uh Groys? Lamplight Dan isn't dead."

"That's why it's so mysterious," said Groys in a loud whisper. "Oh never mind. Let's see. Oh, I know! How about Captain Samuel Salt and the Pacific Northwest Giant Luminescent Freshwater Squid."

Francis' eye lit up like a supernova. He knew it as soon as he heard it. This was it! The jackpot! This was going to win him the contest. He just knew it!

9

THE LEGEND

The wind made the boat creak with every slight back and forth motion from the lake. The full hunter's moon suddenly leapt from behind a cloud, illuminating the lake. Fog slithered through the fir trees that surrounded the lake with a ghostly grace.

Standing atop his fishing boat was Captain Samuel Salt. The old seadog (or in this case lake dog, for Samuel Salt had never actually been to the sea) was relaxing after a day of bountiful fishing with his faithful companion Dusty, his pet crow.

While Cap'n Salt was tying down rig lines, Dusty started cawing over and over again. Cap'n Salt looked up to see what the commotion was about. He noticed a glowing spot out on the lake that he thought at first was just the reflection of the moon. But this was not a reflection. This was something under the water, moving, and toward them.

Soon the glow reached them and the entire boat was surrounded in this strange whitish-blue radiance. Dusty's cawing became more frantic.

Then with lightning speed, a huge tentacle flew out of the water and grabbed poor Dusty. It disappeared again just as fast into the glowing water. The glow retreated back out into the lake and slowly sank from view.

Cap'n Salt stood there shaking with a look on his face somewhere between furious and horrified. After it all sunk in, the dead silence said it all. His best mate for five years was gone. Sinking to his knees, he held his head in his hands and wept for his lost friend. He then rose his head skyward with a defiant shout, cursing whatever abyss the squid came from and vowing that he would send it back there if it was the last thing he'd do. And most likely it would be.

For years after, Cap'n Salt dedicated every waking moment to tracking down that giant, glowing squid. Until, one day, Cap'n Salt was never heard from again. He simply disappeared off the face of the earth.

That was over twenty years ago. Some say he went crazy and drowned himself. Others say he found the squid and sent it back to the abyss where it came from and him along with it. But no one knows for sure what became of either Cap'n Salt or the squid. But some claim that on the full hunter's moon when the fog creeps down through the trees, you can hear Dusty cawing, giving thanks to his master for avenging him and saying good-bye.

10

TO THE LIBRETERY!

"October!" exclaimed Francis. "That's when the hunter's moon is." He stood with a book in his hands entitled, *The Moon Book: A Book about the Moon.*

Francis and the gang were at the local libretery* to look up info on squids, night photography, and atmospheric conditions.

"That's this month," said Ralf.

"Yup, and it's almost over, so we need to get geared up and get out to the lake as soon as possible."

Francis had a fiery look in his eyes that had the others a little worried. But they shrugged it off and continued their research.

Francis had Clyde see if he could find any mention of Captain Samuel Salt in any of the old obituaries from twenty years ago.

After a while, Clyde called out to the rest, and they all came over to the table he was at and looked to where his finger pointed. There was an article about the crazy old captain that said he went missing and was never heard from again. Twenty years ago, someone decided to officially "bury" Captain Samuel Salt.

Clipped to the article was a map and printed on it was the number 42-C. Francis snatched up the map and took off out the back doors and through the iron gates of the cemetery, the rest of the gang in tow.

*The Lamplight Lane Library is also the Lamplight Lane Funeral Home and Cemetery. So the locals have named it the Libretery. The Lamplight Lane forefathers figured since you had to be quiet and respectful at both places, why not just combine the two and save space? Also, as a convenient factor, if a person was to look up in the obituary archives, there would be a plot number and printed map clipped onto it for easy reference.

11

a Cryptic Message of Tall, Grande, and Venti Proportions

Coming to the end of a row of small fir trees there was a smallish hill to the left. At the peak of that hill was a lone crypt with a statue bust adorning the top. Next to it and looming above it like the grim reaper himself was large oak tree, almost a skeleton itself with only a few small clumps of leaves left on it. The rest had fallen on and around the crypt.

Francis and the others walked slowly and solemnly up the hill. The crypt wasn't huge or overly elaborate. It was nicely made with a respectful look. At the top was chiseled: *Samuel Octavius Salt*.

Clyde let out a little snicker that broke the dead silence (pun intended).

"What are you laughing about?" asked Francis in a harsh whisper. For some reason, Francis felt the urge to whisper here, the same feeling he got when in a church, too.

"You guys really don't notice it?" asked Clyde in return.

The boys looked around and then at each other, then finally to Clyde questioningly.

"He was a captain, and his initials are S.O.S.," said Clyde with a smirk.

The others looked at each other and started to snicker too at the irony.

"It's more peculiar then funny," said Francis. He walked up to the crypt and stared at it like he could unravel the enigma that was Captain Samuel Octavius Salt with sheer willpower. He looked down and saw some lettering at the base of the main headstone that was partially covered by leaves. Francis crouched down and brushed them away so he could read the inscription.

Captain Samuel Salt,
He hunted the squid without halt.
For his faithful friend named Dusty,
In an old boat, beat up and rusty.
Now that he is gone
His legend lives on.
Until they clear the way
For a new Starbucks next May.

Francis felt a shiver run down his spine and a sudden rush of sadness after reading that. He also wished he had a nice hot 180-degree soy peppermint mocha latte with whipped cream to warm him up. But he knew it would have to wait until May *and* after he got that photograph. With a triumphant look, he turned to his companions just a few feet away from him. As the first drops of rain started falling, he announced, "Gentlemen, our mission is now of greater importance than the four hundred dollars. It's now also about proving to everyone that Captain Salt wasn't just a crazy old kook, but a passionate individual and loyal friend. We are now obliged to clear his name and make him a true local hero. ARE...YOU... WITH ME?"

The boys looked at each other.

"Wait, what four hundred dollars?" asked Clyde.

THE SQUID COMETH

After explaining the reward money for the contest and his accidental lapse in memory about it, the boys were that much more eager to help Francis. They arrived at the lake with all their gear just before sunset and started setting up their camp site.

The lake stretched out before them and the setting sun made images across it like fireworks dancing on the surface of the water. A cold breeze came through the trees just then and made all the boys jump to put on something warm.

Francis put on his lucky hooded sweatshirt (It wasn't really lucky. It just said the word lucky across it). Clyde turned into a large St. Bernard with layers of warm shaggy fur. Ralf pulled out a large yellow python and draped it around his neck. Palyn produced another rice bag with arm holes and put that on. It wasn't nice to look at, but at least it matched.

After canoeing out a ways, they found a spot that overlooked a great deal of the lake. There they pulled ashore and built a fire to keep warm while they watched.

They began by telling stories and reminiscing of good

times they'd had together. Like when Clyde turned into a stinking, rotting, putrid pile of garbage in the middle of school so that they had to evacuate, thus getting them out of a test. And the time that Ralf commanded a horde of tortoises to eat all the newly sprouted vegetables in the town farms so they wouldn't have to eat any themselves. They all had a good laugh, but as the night progressed, the conversation died off.

Soon the moon rose and was a vibrant red coming over the horizon like an evil eye of a great monster. As it rose higher, the red faded to an orangey yellow. Fog descended upon the lake from the surrounding hills. The boys waited in silence. The only sound was Clyde's whimpers as he dreamed dog dreams and his hind leg twitched randomly.

One by one, the boys were lured by the sandman. Francis was the last to feel the pull of sleep on his eyes. Just as he started to nod, small wakes from the lake started lapping at his feet. He lifted his head at the commotion and saw a most amazing sight.

A huge glowing light was slowly gliding under the dark surface of the water. Francis stood in sleepy shock, watching it move deeper down the lake and around a bend. He snapped out of it and yelled to the others to get up.

The boys jumped up with a, "What? Huh? Woof?"

"I saw it!" shouted Francis. "It was a bright glow under the water, and it disappeared around that bend! Hurry! Get in the boat and let's get after it!"

The boys all scrambled up, jumped into the canoe, and launched it out into the dark lake.

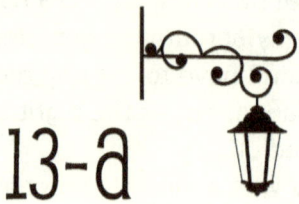

13-a

OF COWARDS, KOLKATA, AND CAPYBARAS

The bright moonlight lit their way as they paddled franticly down the lake. As they rounded the bend, they saw nothing but more darkened lake ahead of them. Not a sign of the glowing squid was to be seen. They drifted out into the middle of the lake, scanning all around for any signs of the animal. Nothing.

"Are you sure it wasn't just a dream, Francis?" asked Palyn.

"Of course I'm sure," said Francis. "It was the squid. It's still here," he said, more to himself than to the others. "It's here. We just need to wait for it to show itself again. We just need to be patient."

The others looked at each other as if in agreement to some prior discussion earlier. They noticed the look in Francis' eyes again and knew they had to intervene.

"Look, Francis," said Ralf, "we think we should head back to camp now. It's probably not the best idea to be out in the middle of a lake at midnight. Plus, its freezing out here. At least we had a fire back at camp. We can just continue the watch there."

"No!" shouted Francis. "This may be our only chance! We can't just give up and go back now." At this, an argument broke out about whether to fish or cut bait. The boy's shouts echoed off the surrounding mountains and trees, resonating across the lake. They were so busy bickering that they didn't even notice the soft glow that was growing directly beneath their boat.

They all stopped at once when the entire area around them was lit with the light from below. Three things happened at that moment.

1. Several gigantic tentacles came shooting out of the water and loomed in the air above them.

2. Someone screamed like a girl (Everyone was pretty sure it was Palyn. Palyn hoped everyone thought it was Clyde).

3. Babot Nahasaraj just took home first place in the extreme skipping championships in Kolkata, India. The latter had nothing to do with the boys, but it happened nonetheless, and I felt it deserved honorable mention.

The tentacles didn't hang there very long before they came down with a fury. The first tentacle came down and across the boat, splintering it in two, sending the boys flying out and into the lake. The remaining tentacles reached for each of the boys, plucking them up and into the air with deft precision.

The boys were freaking out thinking this was definitely their doom. Clyde was so panicked that he changed from the Saint Bernard, to a broom, to a 1967 Mustang convertible, and finally to a terrified screeching Capybara*.

Hanging there in the clutches of the squid, the boys stared in horror as a huge eye surfaced and stared back at them. But something was strange about the monster's eye. It focused on them much like a camera lens. It had the look of something mechanical. After letting the panic settle, they were able to take a good look at the beast and see that it was indeed manmade. The rest of the squid broke the surface and in its side there was a hatch much like the one at Clyde's house. The latch on top turned and the hatch opened.

Capybara: (Pictured above) has a barrel shaped body, webbed toes, and hind legs longer than the front. Their name means "Master of the Grasses", while its scientific name, hydrochaeris, is Greek for "water hog".

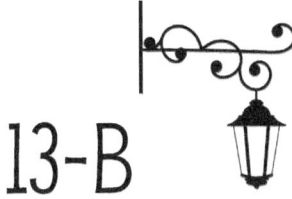

13-B

GESUNDHEIT!*

Out stepped Captain Samuel Octavius Salt.

*To prevent from causing actual brain hemorrhages from the extreme suspense caused by the way the last chapter ended, I decided to just come right out and reveal who was inside the mechanical squid instead of droning on about the mysterious figure that emerged and bantered with the boys about who they were and what they were doing there, thus delaying and prolonging the revealing of the unknown character.

*Gesundheit! (good health to you)

0.0043887689 Leagues Under the Lake

"Burst me bagpipes, boys. I thought ye were poachers or them teens with their great Dane harassin' me again. I almost made haggis out of ye."

"Captain Salt?! Is that really you?" asked Francis.

"Aye, and who be wantin' te know?"

"My name is Francis and these are my friends. We were just out to take a picture of the pacific northwest giant luminescent freshwater squid, for a photo contest. Everyone back in Lamplight thinks you're dead. They even have a crypt in your memory at the Libertery."

"I see. Well it's better that way anyways." The captain looked down with a heavy expression on his face somewhere between great pride and great sadness. "Come now, lads. I'll let ye down and I'll drop ye at the shore line." With that, he climbed back down the hatch and the giant tentacles lowered the boys down and onto the back of the squid. They all scurried down the ladder and into the belly of the beast.

Inside, there wasn't much room. Cap'n Salt had the

helm and the boys just sat on the grated flooring. They watched through the front of the cockpit as Cap'n Salt navigated the squid through the depths of the lake. The illumination of the squid, which was hundreds of soft LED lights strategically placed across the body, cast light around the squid. They glimpsed parts of the lake bed here and there. Among the things they saw at the bottom of the lake were an old fishing boat, a bunch of rusted containers, and an ice cream truck*.

*An innocent bystander of an experiment by the insanely brilliant scientist professor Rubic.

After a bit, the silence grew uncomfortable and Francis spoke up. "Cap'n Salt, sir? What exactly happened to you and Dusty twenty years ago? Was there ever a real squid?"

Captain Salt heaved a great sigh. He cleared his throat and began from the beginning, which was usually the best place to begin.

15

THE LEGEND (TAKE TWO)

"After me first mate was dragged doon to the briney bottom, I vowed te hunt that cursed beast to the ends of the earth!"

"But isn't it confined to just this lake?" asked Clyde

"Ye know what I mean! Stop interrupting me story!"

"Sorry."

"For weeks, I searched for the monster, but ne sign of 'im was te be found. Then the weeks turned in te months, and I'd gi'en up all hope of ever gettin' revenge. But just as the full moon was at its zenith in the sky, the beast showed itself and I took te me boat. I follow'd it round a bend but it disappear'd, and alone I sat in the dark. Then it came up right b'neath me. Great tentacles lashin' out against me. I shot it with me harpoon and it wailed in pain. Then it hauled me up in its great arm only te plunge me b'neath, draggin' me doon with it. Fer hours we were grapplin' together in a final combat to the death!"

"The longest record for being underwater is only 17 minutes and 4 seconds," put in Clyde.*

"Well it seemed like hours! And what did I tell ye!"

"Sorry."

David Blaine holds the Guinness World Record for underwater breath holding at 17min and 4sec.

"Finally, after the gruelin' battle, I had defeated the beast and swam up to the surface as it sank below ne'er te rise again. After that, I suddenly realized I'd probably just killed an endangered species and would be in deep you-know-what if the United States Department of fish and wildlife or Greenpeace found out. So I decided then te build a sub resembling the squid and thus keeping the legend alive as well. But now I've grown accustomed to me new underwater life, and it does feel that I have gone te a better place. I can be closer to me lost mate. So it's with this that I ask ye boys ta not reveal me real where-aboots. Can ye do that for me, lads?"

The boys all looked at each other (and with a silent agreement) they assured the captain's secret was safe with them.

As they stood on the shore watching the cap'n sub-merge and disappear from view, Francis realized he was still holding his digital camera. He turned it on. The screen displayed an amazing photo of the darkened lake with giant glowing tentacles arched up into the sky and the bright full moon directly behind.

16

Preserving a Legend

Seven months later, the boys all met together at the Libertery. They all agreed that the money they won for the photo contest was well spent (Although Francis knew he was a loser and always lost, he realized that he could still be part of a winning team). They stood at the new location of the Captain Samuel Octavius Salt Crypt. Just down the lane from the new Starbucks. Also atop the crypt was another gift from the gang. A life-sized statue of Cap'n Salt's first mate Dusty.

They stood for a moment in thoughtful silence, thinking back to the amazing adventure they had, and of course to Cap'n Salt, wondering if they would ever cross paths with the old Lake Dog again.

Francis turned to face his friends, thinking he should say something profound and wise, but nothing came to mind. So with a toothy grin, he threw one arm around Clyde and the other around both Ralf and Palyn.

"So who's up for a nice 180-degree soy peppermint latte with whipped cream?"

The End

aBOUT THE auTHOr

Darren S. Philibert

Shawn Philibert has loved fantasy and adventure stories ever since his grandmother bought him the Chronicles of Narnia series by C.S Lewis when in middle school. His hobbies include reading (duh) board games and binge watching sci-fi shows. He lives in Eugene, Oregon with his book-loving wife Tara and their dorky cat Stormageddon (Stormy for short)

www.ingramcontent.com/pod-product-compliance
Lightning Source LLC
Chambersburg PA
CBHW020321150626
46552CB00022B/3071